Dora and the Birthday Wish Adventure

adapted by Emily Sollinger
based on the screenplay "Dora Helps the Birthday Wizzle" written by Rosemary Contreras
illustrated by Robert Roper

Simon Spotlight/Nickelodeon
New York   London   Toronto   Sydney

¡Hola, soy Dora! Boots and I are reading a story about a special friend called the Birthday Wizzle.

The Birthday Wizzle lived in Wizzle World and could make all birthday wishes come true with his wishing wand. The Wizzle would see the wish, and just before the birthday candles were blown out, he would say his magic words to make the wish come true: *¡Feliz cumpleaños!* In English we say "Happy birthday!" In Spanish we say *"¡Feliz cumpleaños!"*

One day it was the Wizzle's own birthday. He was excited that it was his turn to make a wish. He wanted to wish for butterfly wings so that he could fly. The Wizzle was just about to make his wish when—*whoosh!* The wind blew the wishing wand out of the Wizzle's hand and right out of the storybook!

¡Mira! The wand is coming to us! We need to catch it and bring it back to the Birthday Wizzle before his candles blow out so he can get his birthday wish.

Let's go to Wizzle World! We just need
to say the magic words. Say it with us:
¡Feliz cumpleaños!

Yay! We made it to Wizzle World! Now how can we find the Wizzle? Who do we ask for help when we don't know which way to go? Map!

Map says the Wizzle is all the way on top of Wizzle Mountain. To get to Wizzle Mountain we have to go through the Unicorn Forest and give a little unicorn her wish. Then we have to go past the Dinosaur Caves and give the twin dinosaurs their birthday wishes.

That's how we'll get to Wizzle Mountain. So remember:
Unicorn, Dinosaurs, Wizzle Mountain.
¡Vámonos! Let's go!

We made it to the Unicorn Forest, but we don't see any unicorns! *¿Donde estan?* Oh! It's raining out, and unicorns don't come out in the rain. They only come out when the rain stops and a rainbow appears in the sky. How can we get the little unicorn to come out so that we can give her a birthday wish?

We'll have to make the rain go away. I know what to say to make the rain go away. You can sing with us! Rain, rain, go away! Come again another day!

We did it! Hooray! The rain cloud is gone, and now there is a big, beautiful rainbow in the sky. And here come the unicorns! The little unicorn is wearing a special birthday crown so everyone will know it's her birthday. She wants to make her birthday wish. Let's help her!

To make her wish come true, we wave the wand and say the Wizzle's magic words. *¡Feliz cumpleaños!* Happy birthday! The little unicorn wished for a new teddy bear!

Next we have to go to the Dinosaur Caves to give the twin dinosaurs their birthday wishes. And we've got to hurry so we can give the Birthday Wizzle his wand back!

The Dinosaur Caves are really far away. Look! I see a train. It's the Birthday Express! We can ride the train to the Dinosaur Caves, and we can give out birthday wishes along the way. Chug-a, chug-a! Chug-a, chug-a! Choo-choo!

We made it to the Dinosaur Caves. Now we need to find the birthday twins. Do you see a cave with a birthday flag on it? The dinosaurs must be in there! But it sounds like the dinosaurs are snoring. We have to wake them up. Let's stomp like dinosaurs. *Stomp! Stomp! Stomp!* Good stomping!

Now the dinosaurs are awake and ready to make their wishes. What are they wishing for? Yeah, a doggy and a robot! We have to say the magic words to give the dinosaurs their wishes. *¡Feliz cumpleaños!*

Hooray! We gave the dinosaurs their birthday wishes. Now we can go to Wizzle Mountain!

We have to make the Birthday Wizzle's wish quickly before his candles go out! Let's say the magic words: *¡Feliz cumpleaños!*

The Wizzle's wish came true! He got his wings. Now he can fly everywhere with his wishing wand and give birthday wishes! The Wizzle is so happy that his own birthday wish came true!

Thanks for coming with us on our adventure and helping us give everyone their birthday wishes! We couldn't have done it without you! *¡Gracias!*